Anonymous

## In Memory of Joseph W. Lester

collection of obituary sermons, sketches and letters

Anonymous

**In Memory of Joseph W. Lester**
*collection of obituary sermons, sketches and letters*

ISBN/EAN: 9783337733957

Printed in Europe, USA, Canada, Australia, Japan

Cover: Foto ©Raphael Reischuk / pixelio.de

More available books at **www.hansebooks.com**

# IN MEMORY

OF

# JOSEPH W. LESTER.

—

AUGUST, 1873.

"Champion of Jesus, man of God,
    Servant of Christ, well done !
Thy path of thorns hath now been trod,
    Thy red cross crown is won."

JOSEPH WILLIAM LESTER was born at Norwich, Conn., September 5th, 1822, and died at his home in New Rochelle, N. Y., August 8th, 1873, in the 51st year of his age.

Mr. SIMEON LESTER, the father of Mr. LESTER, is now 77 years of age. Through him he was a descendant, in about the fifteenth generation, from Sir NICHOLAS LEICESTER, of the County of Cheshire, England, a knight in the thirteenth century.

The family emigrated to New England early in the eighteenth century, and from that time the name was written Lester. They settled in New London County, Connecticut, where some of the descendants still live. The grandfather of Mr. LESTER (WILLIAM LESTER) served in the Revolution, under Col. LEDYARD, at Groton Fort. Fifteen to twenty relatives of the family were killed in the capture of this fort.

Mr. LESTER's father was born in Norwich, Connecticut, in 1796, and in 1825 (Joseph then being a child two years old) moved to New Rochelle, Westchester County, N. Y., where he still resides, an honored elder in the Church, and a bright example of an upright Christian life to all about him. He has been a successful farmer. There were born to him eight children, six boys and two girls, of whom the subject of the present narrative was the oldest. The youngest, DAVID BRAINERD LESTER, is the only child now living. He was associated with his brother in business.

Marked elements in the character of the LESTERS are, persistency in a purpose, and strong adherence to a principle. These characteristics were most prominent in JOSEPH W. LESTER.

The mother of Mr. LESTER was Miss HANNAH MARIA BREWSTER. She was born at Preston, Connecticut, February 6th, 1795, and died at her home in New Rochelle, June 12th, 1865, at the age of 70, after a most exemplary Christian life. Through her, he was a descendant, in the seventh generation, from Elder William Brewster, who came to New England in the " May Flower."

At one time, during the reign of Queen Elizabeth, Elder Brewster was one of the under Secretaries of State. A church was formed in his own house; there they were accustomed to worship, and he was most liberal in its support. This church emigrated to Holland, and afterwards to New England. He was also one of the prime founders of the Plymouth Colony. In all its early history, he was the chief mover in ecclesiastical affairs. As a man, he was social, unobtrusive, enterprising, kind and generous to the poor and godly; he was one of the most popular and efficient men in the Old Colony.

In many of his characteristics, Elder Lester strikingly resembled his renowned ancestor.

[ The following Address was delivered in the Allen Street Presbyterian Church, New York City, by Rev. W. W. NEWELL, D. D., pastor of the Church, December 14th, 1873 ].

I STAND here to-day a stricken mourner. There is a weight upon my spirit; there is a grief in my heart. I feel the awe and solemnity of death. This vacant seat appals me; this absence stuns me; these bereaved relatives and friends oppress me. Our senior elder, our loving and beloved brother, is gone. He has passed the river of death, never to return.

On the 28th of July, I saw Mr. LESTER at his country house in New Rochelle. We all expected his recovery. I went immediately to Grand Isle, in the northern part of Lake Champlain. There I was seriously ill. Late one evening a messenger from the main land handed in a telegram. As I read the fatal words, "Father died last night," I dropped the paper, and sank down under the power of a shock which I shall never forget. It was dark around me.

It seemed like the gloom of that day in August, just six years before, when I was lying by the side of my smitten dead. He and his companion were the first to come to me then. Now, as then, he seemed to be walking at the foot of my bed, saying as he walked, "God has done it, God has done it." I felt that I must go to you. I only asked to sit down among you and share your grief. But I knew that I could not. Oh! the anguish of that night. For almost fourteen years we had loved and prayed and wept and struggled together for Jesus and the lost. In all that time his kindness to me had never wearied; my confidence in him had never wavered. I had tried him in the light and in the darkness. I loved him. I built upon him. I realized what he was to me, to this church, and to the world. With a bound I sprang forward to my life work, inspired by the assurance that he was wishing me God speed.

As the hour of his burial came, I seemed to see the coffined form; the full church and the measured tread, bearing him to the grave. But, dearly beloved friends, there was no lack of mourners; for I learn that firms composed of a hundred men closed their stores, and that five hundred persons went out from the city, and that the people gathered from the surrounding country, reminding us of the prophecy of Amos, "Wailing shall be in all the streets; and they shall say in all the highways, alas! alas!"

This funeral of our brother has called to mind the scene described in the 2d verse of the 8th chapter of the Acts of the Apostles:

"And devout men carried Stephen to his burial, and made great lamentation over him."

And there were certainly resemblances in some of the characteristics of Stephen and our departed brother.

But as my object is not a sermon, but a memorial address, I will make no minute comparisons. I will merely say, in passing, that Stephen was a deacon of the church, who distributed to the wants of the poor. He was a good man, and a man of force, "full of faith and power." He reproved the wicked and stood by the right. He gave his life for the truth, as it is in Jesus ; forgave his enemies, and died a triumphant death.

I am to speak to you now of the life of Mr. LESTER ; not because he needs our commendation, but because we need the stimulus of his example. It will encourage us to find that we may reach after the standard and even attain to some of the characteristics of Stephen, that martyred associate of the Apostles.

Mr. LESTER was a man of tremendous energy, of great promptness of action, and of remarkable persistence. He had a vigorous body, with all the life and spirits of a boy. His industry was prodigious ; yet he never seemed weary. He was the last man whom you would expect to outlive. Gifted with a magnetic power, his manner was so genial and hearty, so cheerful and candid, that people of all conditions were attracted to him.

In January, 1860, I accepted a call to this church. I had traveled alone some 300 miles, in the chill winter. I was full of anxieties for the future. The cars reached the city late in the evening. Long before they stopped, the car door opened, and Mr. LESTER rushed up to me with a greeting so hearty and a welcome so enthusiastic, that my soul was instantly drawn to him; my fears were gone. Swift horses brought us to his cheerful dwelling, where friends were celebrating the anniversary of his wedding. From that day, I have always received at his house the same hearty welcome.

The young people of the church were won to him. He was one of them. Business men were enthusiastic in their admiration of him. Persons with the slightest possible acquaintance were attracted by him.

He was a man of strict integrity and inspired in others the most perfect confidence. He was one whom men loved to name in their wills as guardian of their children or administrator of their estates.

Said an old business friend of his, " Mr. LESTER is my ideal of a man. I have referred to him an hundred times as one whose integrity of heart was so visible in his face, that every person must be inspired with it."

He was a godly man. He was trained to all that was good by an honest, honorable and godly

father, and by a loving, refined and Christ-like
mother; and yet he felt that he must be trans-
formed. He knew that saints might rock his
cradle and that angels might guard his tottering
steps, and yet that he must be born again.

Mr. Christopher R. Robert writes to his wife: "I
remember you and Joseph when you were children;
joyous and happy, but without God. He called you
out of darkness into His marvellous light, leaving
many of your classmates to perish in their sins."

As his whole earth-life and heaven-life hinged
upon this moment of his history, let me add to this
testimony of Mr. Robert, and tell you how he
described the circumstances to me. "I was anxious,"
he said, "about my soul, but saw no way to be
converted. A Christian friend said to me one day,
'Will you serve God?' Yes, with His help, I will.
'Will you give up your sins and trust in Jesus?'
Yes, I do;" and then he added, "From that moment
to this, I have been trying to trust and serve the
Lord." Oh! how simple, how easy this turning
point, and yet how stupendous the results. His
conversion to Christ was not so much a gush of

tenderness as a settled, deep-rooted purpose to fear and love and serve the Lord. Where is the young man that will not do likewise?

Dr. Asa D. Smith, president of Dartmouth College, writes me: "Your letter has touched one of the tenderest chords of memory in my heart. It brings before me afresh those years of our dear departed brother LESTER'S life, with which I was familiar in the old Brainard church. I remember him as a boy in the family of his uncle, that noble servant of Christ, Joseph Brewster. It has always seemed to me that his uncle's mantle fell upon him. When twenty years old he entered our Sabbath School as a teacher, and was soon after converted. The old Brainard church register is before me, and I read: 'JOSEPH W. LESTER, baptized in infancy; received May 28th, 1843.'" His companion united with the church at the same time. "From the vows he then took upon himself, who ever knew him to swerve, in all the thirty years of service that followed? I remember his fidelity to the church. I remember his touching kindness to me in a protracted illness. When my church moved to the Second Avenue, I

was sorry to part with him, but I rejoiced in the
good which I knew he would do in Allen Street.
For frankness and guilelessness, for singleness of
purpose, for earnestness, energy and quiet persistence in his Master's work; for all the qualities that
could render him a help to his pastor and a blessing to the church, I have seldom met his like."

To this striking description of Dr. Smith's, I will
add, that he not only walked in the steps of Joseph
Brewster, his uncle, but, as I have often remarked,
there was a wonderful resemblance between him
and Elder William Brewster, of the "May Flower,"
from whom he was a descendant, in the seventh
generation. They were both remarkable for the
same cheerful, genial manner, and the courageous,
persistent, self-denying devotion to the service of
God, and to the upbuilding of His Church.

"They belonged to Christ's chivalry."

He was remarkable for his general benevolence.
It seemed natural to him to devise liberal things.
It was not only a purpose, but a pleasure. Some-
times he spent more than one-tenth of his yearly

Intuitively alive to signs of suffering, his very presence brought relief and hope.

He was a peace-maker. His good sense and hearty good-will made him very efficient in settling disputes. Though faithful in reproving others, he could acknowledge his own errors. A brother in the church recently said of him, "I never loved that man as I do now. Last evening we differed upon an important matter. This morning he came all this long distance, before breakfast. Taking my hand, in his hearty way, he said, 'I am afraid I spoke too warmly last night. You will forgive it.'"

He was a self-denying, reliable man. "His words were bonds, his oaths were oracles." The business community regarded him as a prompt, energetic, and strictly upright man. The ungodly looked upon him with profound respect. How many a man has said to me, "I would like to be religious, if I could be such a christian as he is." In him religion and business were beautifully harmonized.

He was reliable in his family. Few men ever did more to make home a sweet and well ordered household. How they watched for his well known footstep, and how they were enlivened by his coming. It was a home of culture and comfort, of peace and prayer, of love and hospitality. During almost 27 years, no black cloud ever hung over it. Said his companion to me once, "Our pathway has always been in the sunlight."

He was reliable in the church. He was a pillar there. While such crowds were seeking more congenial homes, he and his united household would not remove from the bounds of the parish. They denied themselves for the church. He died leaving a dwelling within four blocks of this place. His pastor could rely upon his presence and his prayers upon the Sabbath. He had a pleasant greeting and a cordial welcome for strangers in the sanctuary.

He was reliable in the prayer meeting. He was there promptly, and was always ready to take his share of the exercises. He would sometimes do a large business in town, rush out to his country house in New Rochelle, and then come into the prayer meeting without his evening meal. There, forgetting all worldly cares, he would speak or pray with an earnestness and point that was most refreshing. One of the last times he was in that meeting, he spoke of the place as one of the most sweet and precious to him on the face of the earth.

He was reliable in the Sabbath School. Thirty years ago he became a teacher. For a long time he had a flourishing Bible class of young men. For the last eight years he has been a most enthusiastic, popular and successful superintendent of our parish school.

He was reliable as a friend and an adviser. There seemed to be no end to the persons who revealed to him their circumstances and asked his opinion.

For years my companion and myself joined him and his family at the Saturday evening meal. There, after the rush of New York life had subsided, we would spend a delightful hour in social communings and in earnest deliberations about the interests of the church.

But the crowning achievement of his life was his labor for the conversion of men. He was an ardent worker in revivals of religion. The thought of saving the lost fired his soul. It awakened his noblest impulses and his loftiest efforts. To him "the soul of man was larger than the sky and deeper than the ocean." To save that soul was with him a business—a business of transcendent importance. He was anything but an ascetic, or a formalist, or a fanatic. To others he represented the service of God as the most cheerful and honorable thing in the universe. He was judicious. He had such a loathing of all pretences, that he was conservative in reference to revival measures. He approved of the pointed word of God, the power of the Holy Ghost, and such simple measures as the state of feeling demanded. Sometimes he would visit the impenitent in passing home from his day's business. Sometimes the anxious would linger after a service or a prayer meeting; at such times our prayers, instructions and tears were often blessed of God, and we had delightful hope that souls had yielded to Christ. It was in passing away from such scenes, that we experienced together some of the loftiest joys of life. It was almost heaven. Christ and the angels were very near—we could almost catch a strain of joy over repentant souls.

He was cautious in receiving persons into the church from the world.

He was a ministerial man. He did not sustain his pastor in the wrong, but honored his position. In late years, when measures for the promotion of religion were proposed to the session, he would often remark, "The whole field is familiar to our pastor ; I move that it be left to his judgment." In leaving the church on the Sabbath, he would often give his pastor a cheering word in reference to the services. During his illness, he referred with much emotion to the benefit which he himself had received from the Allen Street church.

He was a great man. He had not the fancy or imagination or the literary culture of a poet or a novelist ; but he knew how to deal with men and with things. He knew how to reject shams, and how to cherish realities. His executive ability was remarkable. He was a live man. He seemed to decide things by intuition, and then pressed on his projects with an impetus and a persistence that was sometimes heroic. He was not always right, but he decided well according to the knowledge within his reach.

He had a purpose in life; upon this purpose he concentrated his powers. It was no single performance. He set his face, as a flint, upon the service of God and the benefit of his fellow men, and, with God's help, he has left behind him deep furrows of benign influence. He was a vital force in the right direction. He was a success. This I call great. From small beginnings he built up a large and successful wholesale business. This he transacted for God.

He did his best to sustain his country in the time of her recent struggles.

He was a valued member of many public institutions in this city. Among the seventy or eighty letters of condolence received by his family, are seven from public associations of which he was an efficient officer. The press and the pulpit have commended his life. As chairman of the Financial Committee of the National Temperance Society, he devised liberal things, and gave largely for the promotion of its invaluable work. Besides constant donations to this Society, he gave at one time $1,000, and at another $500. Said the Hon. William

E. Dodge, president of that Society, "We can put a man in his position, but we cannot fill his place."

The Allen Street church is not located among the wealthy and the prosperous. Yet no matter how large the expenses or the contributions, with his help and activity, we always rejoiced at our annual meeting, over a surplus in the treasury.

The Sabbath school that he superintended was a marvel of prosperity. He was a power in the work of leading souls to Christ, and in strengthening the walls of our beloved Zion.

And so, in all this variety of projects he was an efficient helper. Other great men have left their impress on perishable matter. His mark is upon hearts and souls, that never die.

His death was a triumph. He made no special preparation for it. He was not expecting to die. On the 28th of July, just as I was leaving New York for my summer vacation, I went up to New Rochelle. He asked to see me alone. As I entered the room, he said, "You see my body a wreck, but my mind is awake. I have often felt that I needed something more in my religious experience, and I have wondered how it was to come. Three weeks ago this sickness came. I felt that it was all right. My business did not enter my mind. I understood the whole case, and I was entirely ready that God should do his will. Since last Wednesday I was very sick. For three days I did not know how I could get through. Saturday morning I lay here in my weakness, like an infant. I felt as if Jesus took me in his arms and carried me. Somehow, he manifested himself to me in a most *wonderful* way. I never conceived anything like it. My soul was full. It was almost more than I could bear; and now, for three days, I have had a peace and blessedness that I cannot describe. Oh! for one hour of such demonstration of His love as this, I would willingly endure all this sickness. I could not get it myself; He came and gave it to me."

He repeated these and other like words with great rapidity, and as he spoke, the tears were rolling down his face. I stood at his side spellbound. It was a new phase in this dear man's character, and I could only say, "Precious, precious Saviour." It was so like heaven. I knelt at his

bedside. As I closed a brief prayer, he said aloud,
"Amen!" And then came that holy kiss; then our
parting, and that was the last.

Among many other sweet things, he said to his
companion, "God came right to me, and spoke to
me. Oh! I am so happy. I thought I had enjoyed
religion before, but it was a cold service. How
many times have I prayed, especially in revival
seasons, that the Lord would melt my heart, and
now he has burst it. Oh! wonderful, wonderful
love! I want to tell everybody what gladness and
peace I am enjoying."

"In our delightful seasons of prayer," she adds,
"he would say, 'Read me a psalm of praise;' and
as I read, he would say, 'Oh! what a loving Father;
how precious he is to me;' and then as we sang,
'I love to tell the story,' and 'My faith looks up to
Thee,' and 'How sweet the name of Jesus sounds,'
the tears would flow down his cheeks, while he
often exclaimed, 'Oh! how sweet, how sweet!'"

His mother had been dead eight years. During
these manifestations, though never delirious or even
despondent, he said to me, "My dear mother came

to me, and she looked so lovingly into my face, and I looked into her dear, loving eyes; and Jesus also came and stood by me." I said to him, "some would think this a delusion; they would call you a fanatic." "No," said he, "there is no delusion in this, it is too real." I said to him, "I wish I could bear a part of your suffering." "No," said he, "let no one bear it but Jesus." After a painful, sleepless night, he said, "God comes to me so lovingly and says, 'be patient, be patient'—I am willing to bear it for His sake." Through all this he expected to recover. He had such wonderful vitality. He said, "I am not anxious to die; I love my family so dearly, and I have so much to live for. I feel that my work is not done; and if I get well, I shall do *so much more* for Christ." "How more?" I said. "Oh! I shall do it with such a different spirit."

On the 8th, he was visited by his New York physician. He insisted on knowing Dr. Clark's opinion of the case. But he gave him little encouragement. Mr. LESTER immediately dismissed the idea of recovery. He had a conversation with his companion, and soon after said to her mother,

"I have felt that the Lord had more for me to do, but the doctor seems discouraged; and now I would not turn my hand over to decide the matter. I have such a precious Saviour. If He wants me, let Him take me. I have talked with my dear wife, and she bears it like an angel."

The usual time for retiring to rest soon arrived. With a loving kiss and a beaming smile, he said, "Good night, dear wife;" and as she left the room, he said, "Now, mother, I am going to sleep." These were his last words, and this was his last sleep. He soon awoke in heaven. What a sweet and precious ending.

In a few moments his breathing changed. The family were recalled, and there they stood around his bed. But so august was the presence of God in that chamber of death, that not a tear was shed; the tears were to come. As the breath soon left the body, they involuntarily sang, "There are angels hovering round;" and even that wife, after such union of hearts and brightness of life, was enabled to exclaim, "Oh! my dear husband, I would not call you back." The aged father walked the

room, wringing his hands and sighing as he went,
"Why can't I go, why can't I go, in his place?"
But he soon dropped upon his knees before God,
and led them in humble, submissive prayer.

And so, our brother has gone! Gone with
Fanning, Betts, Frazer and Farrel, of the old session. Gone in the prime of his strength, in the
fullness of his zeal, in the vastness of his work.

"He has laid him down at noon, to rest upon his sheaves."

No cloud came over him. The angels bore him
upward, in a blaze of light; the "emerald gates"
were opened and, amid seraph strains, Jesus and
the loved ones gave him welcome. And now he is
at home, amid the rhapsodies of heaven. His great
soul is full at last.

But thousands have said, "Why did he die?"
Die! "Whosoever believeth in me shall never die."
He is not dead. Can he be dead who lives in
glory? Can he be dead whose name is graven on
living hearts? Can he be dead whose life-power
is tramping on in the deeds of living men? The
power of that life will widen and extend. But why
is he gone? This is a hard question to answer.

"Jesus said, what I do thou knowest not now." Look at it as we may, it is a terrible shock. It is an irreparable loss. And yet, we see but in part. "Some things here are veiled: there are many worlds, and much to do." He may be missioned to give us a cheering word or a helping hand. We know that Jesus wanted him. That his death was precious in His sight. That his "pierced hand" has led him, and led him well.

He has achieved wonders. He has done the work of a long life.

"We live in deeds, not years."

He was a hard toiler. He needed rest, and could not get it here. His heart was ever in his work, and so he has gone up higher. May God raise up others to fill his place.

This parting is sad for the wife and the children, the father and the brother, and for all his dear relatives—

"All things round you breathe of him."

You may weep; you may grieve. We will grieve with you. But you must not "lift up for him the voice of wailing." You must not wish him back.

Look forward. "This mortal must put on immortality." The earth shall heave; you shall burst the bars of death. With your spiritual bodies you shall go thronging up together, with such shouts of welcome as are given to victors, coming home. You must come out from the dark cloud, and bask in the sunlight. The noble past is history. It is all done. The golden future is also secure. Thank God for what he has been to you as a husband, a father, a son, a brother. Remember his great delight when his son became a christian, and when his last dear child confessed her Saviour. Remember his beaming smile, his cheerful, loving ways. Then the sweet aroma of his name, and the vital force of his deeds shall never be lost; the ecstasy of his joy shall never cease. How sweet to toil, how sweet to die, while you remember his living and his dying. He longs for your coming. He may be your guardian angel. "He may be near you when the light is low and the heart is sick." And when you cross the river, he may stand upon the other side to cheer you on. With open arms he will give you welcome; once more and forever

you will be together. Till then, be patient, be submissive. Till then—

> "One other comfort, one
> Is yours, to breathe while you adore;
> Thy will be done."

Thus shall your lonely hours be gladdened; thus
shall you "be crowned and sainted."

And now, is there a soul in this house without
God, and with no hope? How firmly he chose the
service of God. He did not defer it. Days and
weeks are rushing on. He did not live in depres-
sion and "die in a panic." He gloried in religion;
it was a blessing to him. Would it not be a
blessing to you? Won't you trust and serve his
Saviour?

And, dearly beloved children, is your noble superintendent gone? Gone to heaven? Do you
remember the last time we saw him together, when
we went down from the May anniversary to our
refreshment room? What a crowd, and how happy
we were; and what a glad, loving speech he made
when he was surprised by that present. Oh! how
he studied and toiled and prayed for you. Listen

now; can't you hear him saying, "Children! won't you love my Jesus? Won't you remember what I told you; and when you are tempted to wrong, won't you, with God's help, resist the devil?"

Young men and young women! how he loved you. He had a heart as young as yours. How he loved to do you good; and how you loved him. How you loved to please him, and how you mourned him. You never will have a friend like him. Don't forget him. Let his presence go with you. Let the power of his life guide you.

Young man, as you sit here to-day, say this in your heart, "As the Lord helpeth me, I will be what he was in the world, in the Sabbath school, and in the labor for souls."

And now, to the officers and members of this church and congregation, and to this crowd of his old friends, rich and poor, let me say, in closing: There has been in our midst a royal life, and a triumphant death; and we would emulate his example. Do you say he was beyond our reach? By no means. His life was not the result of extraordinary power or surprising knowledge or stupendous

exploits. Being blest with great vitality, a vigorous
mind, a good education and a faithful training, he
pressed right on. Nothing deterred him from duty,
and he succeeded because he was eager to do the
most disagreeable things first. And here was one
secret of his wonderfully happy life. He seemed
to be always planning, toiling, succeeding, and he
was doing it for God. There is no pleasure like
constant activity for the honor of Christ and the
good of men. There is joy and heroism in forgetting one's self. Now, what shall our life be?
It is too brief and precious to lose. "It will soon
be dark." The account will end. Then let us—

> "Work away!
> For the Father's eye is on us,
> Never off us, still upon us,
> Night and day!
> Work and pray!"

Why not toil as well as he?

He was not born a saint. Though a frank and
reliable boy, he was yet a sinner. He always had
an impulsive nature. It was hard to restrain his
exuberance of spirits. It was hard for him to bear
with the indolent, the tardy, the unprincipled, the

deceitful. But grace, grace has been working, especially in our revivals of religion.

It was his constant habit to rise early in the morning, and go at once to his little "oratory," where he always prayed, audibly, to God. There he has been heard confessing and renouncing his sins in the deepest abasement, and pleading for others, by name. But he found the blessing; for he often came forth with a radiant countenance and a song of praise; and so, thanks be unto God, he gained the victory. He became gentle and patient and lovely.

Now, if you would live his life, you must have his purpose and prayer, his industry and benevolence, his godliness and love of souls.

If you would have his ecstasies, you must be inspired by his views. In beholding Jesus, you must not only see the scepter in His hand and the crown on His head, but the pity in His heart and the tear in His eye. And if you would die as our brother died, you must climb up to those brilliant heights of heavenly vision where he stood. There your toils and treasures, your gifts and graces, must all be paled in the full-orbed glory of the Cross. There your love of life itself must be absorbed in a supreme attachment to the infinitely blessed God. All this God will give you. Seek it of Him. Then will you honor Jesus and bless your race.

Then will you hail our brother gone, and shine with him, as the stars, forever. And oh! how near that meeting seems. Nothing but the mystic river divides us. We can almost see "the gleam of his snowy robes" and the radiance of his "angel brow." Even now he waits to give us welcome.

[Contributed by Rev. EDWARD R. BURKHALTER, pastor of the Presbyterian Church, New Rochelle].

WHEN those, who in their lives have been marked by rare christian character, pass away from earth, it is most natural and right that some memorial of their name and history should be preserved, as a sweet comfort to their loved ones who survive, and as a guide and stimulus to all whom this memorial shall reach. Mr. JOSEPH W. LESTER was so pre-eminently one of this class—he was so great in goodness—that it is at the same time a sacred duty and a rare privilege to perpetuate his memory. It is true that he was best known, and his influence most deeply felt, in the city, and especially in connection with the Allen Street church; but for the last few years it has been his habit to spend six months of each year in his country home, and here in New Rochelle have we all learned to honor and love him. We have, therefore, our testimony to render and our tribute to bring.

Mr. LESTER said to me in the beginning of my ministry, and often repeated the remark in his own so inimitable manner, "You know that I am better off than most persons, for I have two pastors instead of one." He said it with so much heartiness, and so much depth and sincerity of meaning, that it always gave me a whole world of impulse and encouragement. It was a great and most happy incentive to duty to be called pastor by such a man. Indeed, it could be said of him, that he was a perpetual stimulus to his pastor. He was the most active and useful and zealous layman that I ever knew or ever heard of. Instead of needing, as so many do, the perpetual impulse of the pulpit to keep him in the spirit of christian zeal and diligence, his own constant, warm and active piety reacted on the pulpit, and greatly contributed to keep the preacher in a frame of ardent desire for the welfare of souls. That minister of the Gospel would be a strangely unimpressible man, who could see before him every Sabbath during half the year that face, which was so suggestive of christian labor, and not feel stimulated to preach and pray and strive, with similar ardor, to save souls. But personal contact with Mr. LESTER was most inspiring. There was something quite indescribable about him, which was absolutely contagious. One caught his spirit irresistibly. An interview with him started new thoughts, desires and aspirations in the direction of christian usefulness. Without being at all conscious of it, Mr. LESTER left the impression upon every one's mind that religion was with him the chief concern, the ruling principle; and what was so especially delightful about him, his religion was pre-eminently cheerful, and buoyant, and healthy. This was the case, because religion was with him so eminently practical, and so fruitful of good works. Christianity was not to his mind a treasure to be jealously guarded in one's own soul, as the source of enjoyment in one's secret reflections and meditations: as he understood it, the christian religion is an active and aggressive power—the impulse to do good to one's fellow-men. Religion sent him constantly abroad. He did not tarry long in his own heart, to ponder over its mysteries and perplexities; he went about in every direction doing

good. He believed in doing good of every kind.
He was ready to bring help of every sort, according to the needs which he witnessed. He was a
most sensible and discreet man, and knew well how
to discriminate. He was a good counselor and
friend in both spiritual and temporal matters, and
he always knew in what form to administer his
counsel and his aid.

It was perfectly amazing to learn, (as I have
learned incidentally, from time to time, and I know
that the half has not been told me), how many
persons were reached by his friendly hand, and in
how many directions his sympathies, his interests,
and his active energies, were put forth. I could
scarcely understand how it was possible for him to
keep so many separate interests in his mind, and
to care for them all at the same time. But, amid
them all, no one and nothing were forgotten or
neglected. Although he was so full of thoughts
and cares, because of his interests in the city, there
was a place found in his heart and in his time for
his friends in New Rochelle. I never before understood the capacities of time. I never before knew

that one human life could undertake and accomplish
so much. The secret of it is, he was a man of
unbounded native energy, and there was added to
this a most unusual measure of that mighty principle—love for Christ. These two elements together
made him to be never weary in well-doing.

I cannot forbear adding, that he was also a most
unusual illustration of the application of christian
principle to all the details of life. How he carried
this out in his business I have had no means of
observing, but I have the same assurance as I
should have had I seen it all, that he was a rare
example of business integrity, who in all business
relations never departed from a high christian
standard. But, so far as his life has been led before my eyes, I have observed in it an unbroken
record of the exercise of christian character. His
was a life that manifested the very fewest changes.
As you saw him once, you saw him always. His
sentiments, his convictions, and his principles, were
all established and thoroughly understood, so that
you always knew where you should find him. His
life was disturbed by no fluctuations of feeling, but

when he once assumed a position, he always maintained it. This added great additional value to his character and his influence. You felt that you could always depend upon him. He was sure to be always in his place. We looked for him statedly at our weekly meetings for conference and prayer, although his attendance must have been at the cost of personal inconvenience, on account of his great distance from the church. He was sure to be there, if it was at all possible, and we enjoyed not his presence only, but his cheering and stimulating words.

It can not be my object at this time to give an analysis of Mr. LESTER's character, much less to present any comprehensive view of his worth. That were altogether impossible. In what I have thus written, I have attempted to answer the question, what he has been to me. And let me comprehend it all in closing. He has been to me one of the best and dearest of friends; one of the brightest and most instructive of examples. His memory can never die. His picture, so accurate and so speaking, I keep ever before me, in my study, and I delight to look at it, for it is a perpetual inspiration to me.

It stimulates me to renewed zeal, and constant diligence. It is a perpetual monitor to me, as though his voice spoke to me from out the better world. I believe I can truly say, I am a better and more zealous man for having known and loved Mr. JOSEPH W. LESTER.

# APPENDIX.

" The sun hath set,—
Yet o'er the land still blooms that wondrous glow,
Still shine the topmost peaks, and down below
       The vale is full of light,
       And gloomy night
              Cometh not yet.

       *    *    *    *    *    *

Kindling my inmost soul, still shines Love's day :
       Stronger than Death is Love,—
       From Heaven above
              Heart answers heart."

# SELECTIONS FROM LETTERS AND OBITUARY NOTICES.

---

Cousin Joseph was very dear to us all; he needs no eulogizing. Perhaps I loved him better because in our younger days he was so frank, always reproving me if he saw me in error.

J. F.

LAUREL HILL.

---

I do not think I shall realize that my dear Cousin Joseph has passed away from our earthly sight, until I am in the home that was always so brightened by his presence. How we all felt the influence of his bright, cheering face, as he came into the room. I can only bring him before me in that way now. When I think of him, those lines of Longfellow's often come to me,—

> "O, though oft depressed and lonely,
> All my fears are laid aside,
> If I but remember only
> Such as these have lived and died!"

L. F. B.

CLIFTON, N. Y.

For the last month we have had Joseph continually in
our thoughts. Such a stroke cannot but affect us both, as
for a long time our joys and our sorrows have been so ten-
derly connected. Mere sympathy will help nothing; but if
we speak and think of him as he lived, if we live over the old
days again, holding each tender thought and act close to our
hearts, we can then indeed feel that he still lives. Thank
God we can do this. His look will never die to me.

D. D. E.

---

When I was at your house last winter, Joseph seemed
changed; he appeared more gentle, happier, if possible, and
altogether so lovely in his character, that when I returned
home I spoke to C—— of the change, telling her that it made
me feel that he was living beyond and above us more and
more. That month was a precious one to me, for I remember
his peculiarly happy ways, his greater love for religious work,
his happiness (almost boyish) in the love and attention of the
young men of Allen street. Especially do I remember that
Sunday afternoon, when so many of the young men (I think
there were fifteen) called for him, in order that they might
have the pleasure of walking with him to Dr. Thompson's
Bible class, up town. When Joseph came into the room and
saw the large number who had called for him, and had come
by twos and threes of their own free will, and not by appoint-
ment, then his face was delightful to look upon—he was so
pleased and surprised at seeing them, and their evident love
for him seemed to touch him. I can hear now his happy,
cheery voice, thanking them for calling for him; then his

joyous way of stepping forward and saying, "Come, boys, we
don't want to be late"—speaking to them not as though he
were a dignified leader, but just *one of them* in feeling and
sentiment. Do you remember how we followed them out
just to see that dear brother surrounded by his boys? I
think tears came to the eyes of us both as we spoke of
Joseph's delight in those dear young men, his anxiety for
their welfare and well doing. As he stepped off with his
light, elastic step, I thought who among them all had a finer
physique, a younger heart, a more enthusiastic or fresher
view of life!

There is one thing I aways remember so well, though I
don't know as I have ever spoken to you of it, that is, Joseph's
faithfulness in secret prayer. I have heard him in an adjoin-
ing room, in the early morning, in audible, earnest prayer for
himself and others. I thought them the best prayers he
made. He would speak to God of his great anxiety for his
friends, always mentioning individual cases, and pleading so
earnestly for them. Those who were out of Christ he would
especially plead and pray for; and he prayed as though he
had such trust and reliance in God, that he would hear and
answer his prayers aright. He never neglected his private
devotions, and in leaving would often sing a line or two of
some hymn, such as—

"Come, thou fount of every blessing!"

It is a sad pleasure to recall his dear sayings, and to me his
playful, mischievous ways, are a delight to remember. He
was so alive, so bright, so active—how *can* we realize that he
is gone forever.                                     S. A. D.

No one could see Joseph Lester, much more *know* his worth, without a good and sort of *sacred* influence pervading their whole being. My own respect and love for him were *more* than ordinary. I always looked up to him as an uncommon christian, always ready to depart when the Lord called him. He was my oracle in everything that was good and lovely.

R. B. C.

HARTFORD, CONN.

---

Your husband was doubly dear to me — dear that he was blood kin of one who is so precious to me in memories of her life, dear because he was so much like Him who is the chiefest among ten thousand. Yes, Cousin Joseph bore the image of his Master. Ever since our delightful little visit at N———, in the summer of 1858, I've never ceased to love him. I distinctly remember a little talk he gave us in the church one evening. Some one quoted the familiar passage, " Let me die the death of the righteous, and let my last end be like his !" when he seized it for his text, and spoke so pleasantly and profitably that a lasting impression was made upon my mind, and he seemed to give us the secret of his godly life.

E. T. F.

NEW HAVEN, CONN.

How many mourn with you to-day! The church, the Sabbath school, the prayer meeting, society—all feel the loss. There are few indeed who would be missed more. How precious is the memory he leaves! May the mantle of the father rest upon that dear son. Looking at things from our own stand-point of view, we are ready to say, this good man cannot be spared; the church needs him, the world needs him, society needs him, his family needs him; we cannot have him go yet. But God says to us all, "Heaven needs him;" "shall I not do what I will with my own?" Heaven has become already brighter for a radiant presence newly entered there. *He* has entered into rest, and there is "rest for *you*."

REV. A. R. W.

MONTCLAIR, N. J.

----

We all loved and honored him. Although not privileged to meet him often, we frequently heard his name mentioned, always in connection with some good work, and we know that if it were not that "death loves a shining mark," he would have been spared to love and bless you with his presence. And now you and your dear children are heirs of the gospel of his precious life, a legacy which any might covet.

M. C. H.

Very few, my dear friend, have enjoyed the enviable lot which has been yours for a quarter of a century. It is the happy lot of but few women to have *such* a companion — so pure and good a man, so noble a christian character. Truly the mantle of his sainted uncle fell upon him. They were lovely in their lives, blessed in their deaths, and their works do and will follow them.

O! how many, many besides myself have occasion to-day to go back and recall the generous acts of christian kindness received at his hands. How many poor will weep in secret places, how many young persons whom he has led to Jesus, how many warm christian hearts whom he has comforted and encouraged.

How many christian ministers, who have enjoyed the privilege of his friendship, can say, as my heart has been continually saying, " Very pleasant, my brother, hast thou been unto me."

REV. V. LE R. L.

NEW YORK MILLS, N. Y.

---

I have lost my truest friend, the man to whom I owe more as a minister, and Port Huron church owes more as a band of Christ's followers, than to any other person.

His energy, his industry, his economy, his beneficence, his charity — all told in the formation of my ministerial character. His consecration to Christ was the clearest instance I had ever met, and I have never met another like it since.

And now, not boastingly, the church at Port Huron has the name of being the most wide-awake, and in truly christian giving, the most liberal Congregational church in the State of Michigan. So he lives in me, in my church, and in the churches of the State. Oh, how a man sows himself into the soil of centuries when he works for Jesus. Oh, that I may feel, as I think of going, that I have done as much as I think he has done. But the very best of his friendship I consider to have been, that stern sense of demanding of me what was right, and reproving what was wrong, even though it were but omission. That evening when first he came to see me at Union Theological Seminary! Oh, it shaped my whole ministerial life as an active and patient one, and made me love the work of saving souls as nothing else has. He is my god-father indeed.

REV. J. S. H.

PORT HURON, MICH.

---

There was no *friend*, not one, that I loved more than Joseph Lester, and I felt honored by *his* friendship. As a *christian* brother, I loved him—so true, so humble, yet so firm and resolute. "I have kept the faith" may well be written of him. *We* lose his cheering words and his devoted life, his prayers and his generous sympathy, and the love of his big, warm heart; but *Heaven* gains it all, and it will be happier there (if such a thing were possible) with him among them. "His works do follow him;" yes, they have gone

before him, and will be his diadem forever. It almost seems
to me I can hear, among the voices that have greeted him,
one that is saying, " Well done !"

This is not all. The *memory* of Joseph Lester is precious,
and it will live when hundreds are forgotten.

J. P. P.

———

To know your husband was to love him. I always loved
to meet him and have a friendly talk. I don't know of any
one, not even a brother, who had my confidence more than
your husband. He was always cheerful and pleasant, never
complaining or desponding, but looking always on the bright
side and feeling hopeful.

O. B. J.

Lake George, N. Y.

———

I had known and loved him many years, when we were
brought more closely together by meeting every month in
the Board of Managers of the National Temperance Society.
He, like myself, was scarcely absent from those meetings,
and we were always of one mind, in everything that con-
cerned a cause he had so much at heart. We will greatly
miss him and his wise counsels in that Board. There was
no other member in whose sound judgment I had such
implicit confidence. I scarcely see how we are to get on
without him.

His plain, unassuming ways, his unselfishness, his thoughtfulness for others, his willingness to work and readiness to contribute—all endeared him to us more than I can express.

P. C.

———

He was my friend—I esteemed him highly: not alone because he was my friend in all times of business cares, but because he was a self-made man, upright and honorable in all his dealings, and with a heart which was always ready to sympathize with others in need.

W. S.

CHARLESTON, S. C.

———

Truly he was a most extraordinary man—most unusually christian, most singularly wise and good, strong, loving and tender. He was universally esteemed, respected and beloved. You would be comforted, indeed, did you know what an impression he has left upon the hearts of all of us at New Rochelle.

I feel the most perfect assurance that the impression he has left upon my heart will never be lost, and I would count it one of my greatest blessings if it could be kept as vivid as it is now. I pray that it may be.

REV. E. R. B.

MANCHESTER, VT.

It seems but yesterday that I met him, and had the usual cordial grasp of the hand and the kindly word and smile. We were nearly of an age, and have taken " sweet counsel together" for many years. If to live so as to be missed be an object for the christian, surely he early attained it. How he will be missed in the circle of his business friends, in the Church of Christ, and in the sacred circle of his own family. He leaves few equals behind him.

W. C.

———

In all these years since I first met your husband, I have not met the man whom I more honored and loved, as a sympathizing, consistent christian man. Oh, how blessed to have so lived and died.

Rev. J. H. T.

Lake Forest, Ill.

———

I never before felt more seriously the loss of a friend than in the departure of almost my dearest friend, Mr. Joseph W. Lester. He has been as a ministering angel to me, ever since the first Sabbath morning that I went into your Sunday school, in Allen street. He met me so cordially and made me feel so much at home, took such pains to introduce me to the teachers and superintendent, and afterwards invited me to sit with him in your pew ; and, if I remember aright, took me home to dinner, then to Sunday school again, to Young Peoples' prayer meeting, and to evening church. His kindness and largeness of heart have been manifested in so many ways, and so frequently, that no language that I can command will convey any proper conception of my esteem and admiration for him as a *christian man*, in the true sense of the term.

Mr. Lester has been a great blessing in the church, Sunday school, prayer meetings, benevolent associations, Bible and tract societies, American S. S. Union, and, not least by any means, as a christian merchant, who was not ashamed to show his true colors in his counting-room. His associations in these different relationships have brought him in contact with a host of individuals, and God only knows the ultimate results of influences set in motion or owing their origin to Mr. Lester.

H. P. A.

Philadelphia, Pa.

––––––

Though I knew Mr. Lester was a mighty worker, yet I presumed he possessed vigor equal to the tax levied daily upon his system; and I have always anticipated a hale and hearty old age for him. But what he would not accord to himself, the Lord has given to him—REST! Now he has entered into the full enjoyment of " Rest, Refuge and Home."

Whenever my thoughts wandered to New York, I always remembered Mr. Lester as a much prized friend. I always felt better for meeting him. How much I shall miss him! He was a model christian business man. His christianity was felt under all circumstances. He daily proved that a man can be a thorough christian, and successful in business at the same time.

The energy displayed in the store was given also to the work of the church. He was a tower of strength to his pastor—such a co-laborer as any minister would be proud to possess. Many will arise to call him blessed, and who can estimate the number of stars in his crown of rejoicing? I have gone over in imagination the hundreds of different persons for whom he has made life sweeter, and across whose pathways he has thrown a ray of sunlight.

To be a minister of good cheer is to be a minister of God; and such a man was Mr. J. W. Lester. May the Lord grant to business circles and to the church many such men.

REV. N. B. R.

TROY, N. Y.

———

[ From a Sunday School Scholar ].

You know Mr. Lester was an exemplary man in all respects, therefore we looked to him for an example more than we ought: also, the rest of the church folks let him do too much of the work, and were too dependent on him, not only for money but also to do almost all the thinking. Now, somebody else must do the thinking and acting, and there will be more than one who will be willing to work for Jesus, and thereby obtain a starry crown. It seems as though at the mention of Mr. Lester's name, the young men are inspired, and I wish you could hear some of them speak, and hear their resolves to work with a will and build up the church by their united efforts.

LILY M.

O, how I have felt since dear Mr. Lester's death. I cannot express my loss. In him I have lost the only father I ever knew, for indeed he has been a father to me for thirteen years.

I love to think of him as having been the means of leading hundreds to Christ. No one ever left the world of whom it could be more appropriately said than of him—"I have fought a good fight, I have kept the faith: henceforth there is laid up for me a crown of righteousness."

H. P. T.

Portland, Me.

I can say honestly, that after my only brother, no man living had such a hold of my heart as Mr. Lester.

How many times he has interested himself in my behalf. I remember one case. One night I came to prayer meeting, jaded, worried, worn out; my face (which with me is always a tell-tale) told the story. Our minister called upon me the very first to engage in prayer. I had to comply in a few feeble utterances. Some three months after, in conversation, the subject was touched, and I expressed surprise that in my miserable state, I should have been called upon, at that time. Mr. L. replied, " Man, my sympathies were more drawn out and excited by that helpless, broken-up prayer of yours, than any I ever heard you present!"

Panegyrics upon those who have departed, are at best, in most cases, a tissue of misrepresentations; but the half of the truth, as I can testify, was not told in regard to him.

The humble christian, the faithful friend, the true citizen— not to say anything of his own private home virtues, were all *united in him.*

H. G. F.

PARIS, FRANCE.

# OBITUARY NOTICES.

[From the *New York Observer*, August 21st, 1873].

Viewed from a christian stand-point, Joseph W. Lester was no ordinary man. He was a bright, shining light in the Church of Christ, to which his whole life from early manhood was singularly devoted. His entire life was freely spent in his divine Master's cause. Hundreds of the poor of New York, who came within the sphere of his charmed circle of usefulness, can bear testimony to the fact that his hand was ever open to the wants of the needy, many if not all of whom he led, by his winning, gentle manner and persuasive eloquence, to the feet of Jesus, and who now rejoice in His saving grace. It is impossible to do anything like justice to the character of Mr. Lester in an obituary notice. To speak of his christian graces and many acts of christian charity would fill a volume. Truly can it be said of him, he "fought a good fight" and "kept the faith," and is now wearing that crown of righteousness reserved for the valiant soldiers of the Cross.

[ From the *National Temperance Advocate*, September, 1873 ].

Mr. Lester had been a member of the Board of Managers
of the National Temperance Society since its organization,
and was, at the time of his death, chairman of the Finance
Committee.

He was one of the most efficient members of the Board;
always prompt, ready with judicious counsel, genuine sympathy and generous material aid.  Much of the success and
usefulness of the National Temperance Society and Publica-
tion House has been due to his hearty co-operation and
valuable, though unostentatious, labors in connection with
the management of its financial affairs.  He will be sadly
missed and mourned by his associates, and by all who knew
him.  The temperance cause can ill afford, at the present
juncture, to lose so staunch and steadfast a supporter and
worker.

[ From the *Sunday School Times*, September 6th, 1873 ].

Joseph W. Lester, our beloved superintendent, is dead.
A good man, a great man has fallen.  As superintendent
of the school—Allen Street Presbyterian—we deplore his
loss, and cannot fill his place.  Punctual, practical, kind,
loving, sympathizing, with a pleasant word for every one,
he was loved by all, to the youngest of the infant class,
He was modest, humble, abounding with " charity towards
all," benevolent beyond others.  He was a godly man, and

in his closet received the strength which he asked of God, and would come forth with countenance beaming, ready for his work, and equal to any emergency.

When the pinching cold of winter comes, the poor of the church will miss him; "For," said one of the deacons, "wherever I went I found that his footsteps had been before me." He was the wise counselor in the Eldership. He has led us as a church for years past "out of the depths" (pecuniarily) when "deficiencies" have been either large or small.

Always in his place in the social prayer meeting, his exhortations — short, pointed, earnest — carried conviction to all who heard them: how many who said, "It did me good to hear him talk." If we turn to business, we hear the same story. Mr. Lester was a *superior* business man, and was prospered of God. We believe that as he gave away he "increased." Many young men attribute their success in business — some entirely, some largely — to him. Some he established, others aided materially, others assisted by sound judgment and advice.

Let us emulate his virtues, and follow him as he followed Christ.

---

[ From *The Hat, Cap and Fur Trade Review*, September, 1873 ].

The trade has suffered a great loss by the death of Joseph W. Lester, who leaves behind him an untarnished name and reputation. He was essentially a good, worthy citizen. Hard working and a thorough business man, he never for a moment forgot that life has other duties besides mere money-making, and so devoted himself to every effort that conduced to elevate his fellow-men. Such an existence has to us a special charm. There is a straightforward, honest manliness about it that soars above the miserable pettiness of our every-day life, and in our opinion does, single-handed, more to improve the general welfare than all the ill considered efforts of those who indulge in spasmodic fits of benevolence and religion. No higher and nobler testimony of Mr. Lester's usefulness can be given than the following paper which, at his death, was circulated among the trade:

In consequence of the death of our esteemed fellow-citizen, Joseph W. Lester, Esq., whose loss we so sincerely deplore, and in testimony of our respect for his exalted worth as a man, his usefulness as a citizen, his unbending integrity as a merchant, and his amiable qualities as a friend, we, the undersigned, manufacturers and wholesale hat dealers, agree to withdraw from our labors for the day, and to close our respective places of business, at the hour of 1 o'clock, on Tuesday, the 12th instant, for the purpose of attending his funeral, to be held in the Presbyterian church, at New Rochelle, at 2 o'clock, P. M.

[SIGNED BY FIFTY-ONE FIRMS].

---

[ From the *New York Evangelist*, August 21st, 1873 ].

Rarely is a community called to mourn the loss of so estimable a citizen as Joseph W. Lester.

A man of untiring industry, strict integrity and of economical habits, he soon attained the front rank in his calling, and acquired a competency. While his counting-room has found him assiduous in the discharge of its daily duties for years past, the fruits of his efforts have been liberally disseminated among benevolent objects in unostentatious charity. Recognized as a most exemplary merchant while living, none could be more lamented in death. Few have succeeded in establishing a reputation so spotless and a character so lovely.

Identified as he had been with the interests of the wholesale hat trade, and brought into daily intercourse with its members for more than a quarter of a century, none knew better how to estimate his virtues or appreciate his worth. His was a character which commanded the respect, love and confidence of all classes and conditions of men. His was a christianity which reflected from within the holy emotions of a pure and exalted faith, practically illustrating in daily life the essence and value of true religion. Scrupulously punctilious in all his engagements, the important and minor details of his business were conducted upon the strictest principles of rectitude and honor. His was a life that embellished the counting-room, dignified his calling, sweetened intercourse, and indelibly impressed the beauty and influence of a holy example upon the minds of his associates. Unassuming, meek, gentle, affable, modest and refined, with a kind word for all, his relations with business men have left recollections of the most pleasing and happy character. We love to think of him as we saw him daily moving, with quick, elastic step, countenance radiant with inward joy, and smiles of friendship which we knew were pure, because reflected from a heart that knew no guile. In him were clustered irresistible graces, which while they inspire love, magnetize and charm.

Though his spirit has passed beyond that bourn from whence no pilgrim returns, his influence still lives, while the recollections of his virtues are enshrined in heart and embalmed in memory.

Press of C. H. Jones & Co., 114 Fulton Street, New York City.